奥斯卡·王尔德 1854年10月16日生于爱尔兰都柏林。英国唯美主义的代表作家、童话作家和剧作家。著有小说《道连·格雷的画像》、童话《快乐王子》、书信《自深深处》，以及剧作《莎乐美》《温夫人的扇子》等。1900年11月30日，在巴黎的一家旅馆里，王尔德因脑膜炎去世，终年四十六岁。

李玉瑶 译者、编审，现任职于上海译文出版社。译有《传家之物》《快乐影子之舞》《岛上书店》《房间》《玛格丽特小镇》《与狼共舞》《激情》等二十余部作品，其中《传家之物》荣获2018书业年度评选年度翻译奖。

光尘
LUXOPUS

[英] 奥斯卡·王尔德 著　　＼　　李玉瑶 译　　迷人的气质

上海文艺出版社

OSCAR

WILDE

1

《温夫人的扇子》
Lady Windermere's Fan

满嘴仁义的男人通常伪善,张口廉耻的妇人必定无趣。

**A man who moralizes is usually a hypocrite,
and a woman who moralizes is invariably plain.**

2

女人是用来疼爱的，而非用来理解的。

Women are meant to be loved, not to be understood.

《没有秘密的斯芬克斯》
The Sphinx Without a Secret

3

《无足轻重的女人》
A Woman of No Importance

当好丈夫的男人乏味得可怕,不是好丈夫的男人则自负得卑劣。

Men are horribly tedious when they are good husbands, and abominably conceited when they are not.

哭泣是寻常女子的避难所，却是漂亮女人的滑铁卢。

Crying is the refuge of plain women but the ruin of pretty ones.

《温夫人的扇子》
Lady Windermere's Fan

5

《身为艺术家的评论者》
The Critic as Artist

人行事时是木偶，一开腔就成了诗人。

When a man acts he is a puppet.
When he describe he is a poet.

6

《无足轻重的女人》
A Woman of No Importance

坏男人钦慕纯真,坏女人则让男人无法自拔。

**A bad man is the sort of man who admired innocence,
and a bad woman is the sort of woman a man never gets rids of.**

7

《温夫人的扇子》
Lady Windermere's Fan

男女之间不可能存在友谊。有爱恨情仇,但绝无友谊。

Between men and women there is no friendship possible. There is passion, enmity, worship, love, but no friendship.

8

《不可儿戏》
The Importance of Being Earnest

花容月貌是每个聪明男人都心甘情愿投身的罗网。

Good looks are a snare that every sensible man would like to be caught in.

9

《无足轻重的女人》
A Woman of No Importance

**我认为世上没有女人被求爱时会不觉得受宠若惊，
而这使她们可爱到让人无力招架。**

**I don't think there is a woman in the world who would
not be a little flattered if one made love to her.
It is that which makes women so irresistibly adorable.**

绝世美女的丈夫皆属犯罪阶级。

The husbands of very beautiful women belong to the criminal classes.

10

《道连·格雷的画像》
The Picture of Dorian Gray

11

《无足轻重的女人》
A Woman of No Importance

一个男人长大到足以把事情做错,他也应该长大到足以把事情做对。

When a man is old enough to do wrong he should be old enough to do right also.

12

——《温夫人的扇子》
Lady Windermere's Fan

当男人绝口不再提某样东西迷人时,
他们也就认为这样东西魅力不再。

When men give up saying what is charming,
they give up thinking what is charming.

13

《无足轻重的女人》
A Woman of No Importance

断不能相信透露自己真实年龄的女人。
连这都据实以告的女人是无所不言的。

One should never trust a woman who tells one her real age.
A woman who would tell one that, would tell one anything.

除非你紧追不舍,否则她永远不会爱上你:
女人就喜欢被纠缠。

She will never love you unless you are always at her heels: women like to be bothered.

——《薇拉》 Vera

15

《无足轻重的女人》
A Woman of No Importance

寻常女子总在猜忌自己的老公。
美女们可压根儿没这工夫。
她们一直忙着猜忌别人的老公呢。

Plain women are always jealous of their husbands.
Beautiful women never have time.
They are always so occupied in being jealous
of other people's husband.

往事的魅力就在于其已成往事，
可女人们从不知道何时落的幕。

**The one charm of the past is that it is past.
But women never know when the curtain has fallen.**

《道连·格雷的画像》
The Picture of Dorian Gray

17

《理想丈夫》
An Ideal Husband

她看上去像个有阅历的人,漂亮女人大抵如此。

She looks like a woman with a past. Most pretty women do.

18

《帕都瓦公爵夫人》
The Duchess of Padua

唯有惊世丑女或绝世美女才会掩藏自己的面容。

It is only very ugly or very beautiful women who ever hide their faces.

19

《理想丈夫》
An Ideal Husband

终其一生,女人真正的悲剧只有一个。
那就是,过去永远归于她的情人,
而未来一成不变地隶属于她的丈夫。

**There is only one real tragedy in a woman's life.
The fact that her past is always her lover,
and her future invariably her husband.**

我喜欢有故事的女人。跟她们交谈总是乐趣无穷。

I prefer women with a past.
They are always so damned amusing to talk to.

—— 《温夫人的扇子》 Lady Windermere's Fan

21

《道连·格雷的画像》
The Picture of Dorian Gray

女人总想要爱情天长地久,而正是这份努力毁掉了所有的爱情。

They spoil every romance by trying to make it last forever.

朝三暮四和终身不渝之间的区别仅在于前者维持得更久一些。

The only difference between a caprice and a lifetime passion is that the caprice lasts a little longer.

《道连·格雷的画像》
The Picture of Dorian Gray

23

《对话》
In Conversation

我偶尔会揣测,上帝在造人时,多少高估了他自己的能力。

**I sometimes think that God in creating man,
somewhat overestimated His ability.**

男人因为厌倦步入婚姻，女人出于好奇披上婚纱，
而双方皆大失所望。

Men marry because they are tired; women because they are curious;
both are disappointed.

《道连·格雷的画像》
The Picture of Dorian Gray

25

《道连·格雷的画像》
The Picture of Dorian Gray

婚姻的显著缺点在于使人变得无私起来。
但无私之人都寡淡呆板,缺乏个性。

The red drawback to marriage is that it makes one unselfish.
And unselfish people are colorless.They lack individuality.

倘若我们男人娶了个自己配得上的老婆，
日子可就非常不好过了。

If we men married the women we deserved,
we should have a very bad time of it.

《理想丈夫》
An Ideal Husband

27

《无足轻重的女人》
A Woman of No Importance

二十年的韵事会让一个女人犹如一座废墟，
二十年的婚姻则使她好似一幢公共建筑。

Twenty years of romance make a woman look like a ruin;
but twenty years of marriage make her look like a public building.

婚姻生活中,夫妻间彻底厌恶对方之时即爱意降临之际。

In married life affection comes when people thoroughly dislike each other.

《理想丈夫》
An Ideal Husband

29

《无足轻重的女人》
A Woman of No Importance

没有什么比女人有幽默感——
或男人没有幽默感——更能破坏一段恋情。

**Nothing spoils a romance so much as a sense
of humour in the woman – or the want of it in the man.**

不论经历何种浪漫史，最糟糕的是让人浪漫不再。

The worst of having a romance of any kind
is that it leaves one so unromantic.

30

《道连·格雷的画像》
The Picture of Dorian Gray

31

《了不起的火箭》
The Remarkable Rocket

真爱艰辛而隐忍。

True love suffers, and is silent.

男人总想当女人的初恋,这是他们拙劣的虚荣心使然。
女人更为细腻地洞察世事,她们想要成为男人最后一段浪漫史。

Men always want to be a woman's first love.
That is their clumsy vanity.
Women have a more subtle instinct about things.
What they like is to be a man's last romance.

《无足轻重的女人》
A Woman of No Importance

《夜莺与玫瑰》
The Nightingale and the Rose

**爱情是多么愚昧！没有逻辑来得一半有用，
因为爱情什么都证明不了，还总是告诉世人不可能发生的事，
并让他们相信莫须有的东西。**

**What a silly thing love is! It is not half as useful as logic,
for it does not prove anything and it is always telling
one things that are not going to happen and making
one believe thing that are not true.**

一个亲吻可能毁掉一个人的一生。

A kiss may ruin a human's life.

《无足轻重的女人》
A Woman of No Importance

35

《道连·格雷的画像》
The Picture of Dorian Gray

凡是他不爱的女人，男人都可以与之愉快相处。

A man can be happy with any woman as long as he does not love her.

恋爱时，人以自欺欺人为始，以欺骗他人告终，
而这就是世人所谓的爱情。

When one is in love one begins by deceiving oneself,
and one always ends by deceiving others.
That is what the world calls a romance.

《无足轻重的女人》
A Woman of No Importance

37

《道连·格雷的画像》
The Picture of Dorian Gray

年轻男子有心忠诚,却身不由己;
老年男人有意不忠,却力不从心。

**Young men want to be faithful and are not;
old men want to be faithless and cannot.**

忠贞不二的人只了解爱情琐碎的一面；
见异思迁者才懂得爱的悲辛。

Those who are faithful know only the trivial side of love:
it is the faithless who know love's tragedies.

《道连·格雷的画像》
The Picture of Dorian Gray

39

《自深深处》
De Profundis

欢愉遮蔽了爱,痛苦却揭示了爱的本质。

Pleasure hides love from us but pain reveals it in its essence.

人人都值得爱,除了那个自以为值得的人。

Everyone is worthy of love, except him who thinks that he is.

《自深深处》
De Profundis

41

《无足轻重的女人》
A Woman of No Importance

人应该永远恋爱。这就是人应该永远不结婚的理由。

One should always be in love.
That is the reason one should never marry.

我不喜欢结局圆满的小说。这种小说让我丧气。

I don't love novels that ends happily. They depress me so much.

《不可儿戏》
The Importance of Being Earnest

《不可儿戏》
The Importance of Being Earnest

我一向认为,意欲结婚的男人若非无所不知,就是一无所知。

I have always been of opinion that a man who desires to get married should know either everything or nothing.

我揣测,男人一旦爱过一个女人,
他就凡事都愿意为其效劳,但继续爱她除外?

I suppose that when a man has once loved a woman,
he will do anything for her, except continue to love her?

《理想丈夫》
An Ideal Husband

45

《婚姻手册》
A Handbook to Marriage

婚姻是一个所有女人皆赞同、全体男人尽反对的议题。

**Marriage is the one subject on which
all women agree and all men disagree.**

我们所处的这个时代,人们把艺术视为一种自传。

**We live in an age when men treat art
as if it were meant to be a form of autobiography.**

《道连·格雷的画像》
The Picture of Dorian Gray

47

《社会主义制度下人的灵魂》
The Soul of Man Under Socialism

艺术家是相信自己的人,因为他绝对自我。

**The artist is a man who believes in himself,
because he is absolutely himself.**

讨厌艺术的方式有两种……一种是单纯地讨厌它，
另一种是理性地喜欢它。

**There are two ways of disliking art ... One is to dislike it.
The other is to like it rationally.**

《身为艺术家的评论者》
The Critic as Artist

49

《道连·格雷的画像》
The Picture of Dorian Gray

我们这个年代的人书读得太多而头脑糊涂，
思考得太多而样貌丑陋。

We live in an age that reads too much to be wise,
and that thinks too much to be beautiful.

唯有浅薄之辈才不以貌取人。

It is only shallow people who do not judge by appearances.

《道连·格雷的画像》
The Picture of Dorian Gray

《理想丈夫》
An Ideal Husband

昨晚她浓妆艳抹,几乎衣不遮体。这往往是女人陷入绝望的迹象。

**She wore far too much rouge last night and
not quite enough clothes.
That is always a sign of despair in a woman.**

人畜无害的理念根本不配称为理念。

An idea that is not dangerous is unworthy
of being called an idea at all.

《身为艺术家的评论者》
The Critic as Artist

53

《供年轻人使用的至理名言》
Phrases and Philosophies for the Use of the Young

人应当要么成为一件艺术品,要么穿戴一件艺术品。

One should either be a work of art, or wear a work of art.

最糟糕的作品总是源于最美好的初心。

It is always with the best intentions that the worst work is done.

《身为艺术家的评论者》
The Critic as Artist

55

《不可儿戏》
The Importance of Being Earnest

每当有人跟我聊起天气,我总觉得他们肯定别有用心。

**Whenever people talk to me about the weather,
I always feel certain that they mean something else.**

真正魅力四射的人只有两种——无所不知者,以及一无所知者。

There are only two kinds of people who are really fascinating – people who know absolutely everything and people who know absolutely nothing.

《道连·格雷的画像》
The Picture of Dorian Gray

《对话》
In Conversation

守时是时间的窃贼——我自己不是个守时的人,
可是我很喜欢别人守时。

Punctuality is the thief of time – I am not punctual myself,
but I do like punctuality in others.

登门造访者为的是浪费别人的时间，而非自己的。

When one pays a visit it is for the purpose of wasting other people's time, not one's own.

《理想丈夫》
An Ideal Husband

59

《理想丈夫》
An Ideal Husband

有客来访时我自己坐的那把椅子是最舒服的一把椅子。

The most comfortable chair is the one
I use myself when I have visitors.

哦,真高兴你来了。千头万绪我啥也不想对你说。

Oh, I'm so glad you've come.
There are a hundred things I want not to say to you.

《对话》
In Conversation

60

61

《道连·格雷的画像》
The Picture of Dorian Gray

世上只有一件事比被人议论更惨,那就是没人议论。

There is only one thing in the world worse than being talked about, and that is not being talked about.

谋杀总是错的……凡是不能在茶余饭后拿来闲聊的事情都不该做。

Murder is always a mistake ... One should never do anything that one cannot talk about after dinner.

《道连·格雷的画像》
The Picture of Dorian Gray

63

《理想丈夫》
An Ideal Husband

我通常都心口如一。当今,这可是个大毛病,很容易遭人误解。

**I usually say what I really think. A great mistake nowadays.
It makes one so liable to be misunderstood.**

八卦人人爱！历史不过就是八卦。
而丑闻则是被仁义道德搞得乏味无趣的八卦。

Gossip is charming! History is merely gossip.
But scandal is gossip made tedious by morality.

《温夫人的扇子》
Lady Windermere's Fan

65

《温夫人的扇子》
Lady Windermere's Fan

我喜欢对着砖墙说话，那是世上唯一永远不会跟我抬杠的东西。

**I like talking to a brick wall,
it's the only thing in the world that never contradicts me.**

像我这种想要聊聊自己的人，就恨你们这种总爱讲自己的人。

I hate people who talk about themselves, as you do,
when one wants to talk about oneself, as I do.

《了不起的火箭》
The Remarkable Rocket

67

《身为艺术家的评论者》
The Critic as Artist

人们在道旁人长短时通常索然无味,而聊起自己时往往趣味横生。
倘若他们能在令人烦倦前就闭上嘴,
就像一本看厌了的书被轻易合上,那他们就尽善尽美了。

When people talk to us about others they are usually dull.
When they talk to us about themselves they are nearly
always interesting, and if they could shut them up,
when they become wearisome, as easily as one can shut up a book
of which one has grown wearied, they would be perfect absolutely.

每当别人赞同我的观点,我总觉得自己肯定是错了。

When people agree with me I always feel that I must be wrong.

《温夫人的扇子》
Lady Windermere's Fan

《无足轻重的女人》
A Woman of No Importance

不要对自己的坏毛病太自负。随着年岁渐长,你连这些都会失去。

**Don't be conceited about your bad qualities.
You may lose them as you grow old.**

除了天气,我不想改变英国的一丝一毫。

I don't desire to change anything in England except the weather.

《道连·格雷的画像》
The Picture of Dorian Gray

71

《理想丈夫》
An Ideal Husband

听人讲话是件非常危险的事。只要聆听就可能被说服，
而甘愿被辩论说服的人是根本不可理喻的。

It is a very dangerous thing to listen.
If one listens one may be convinced;
and a man who allows himself to be convinced
by an argument is a thoroughly unreasonable person.

我讨厌任何一种争论。争来辩去向来粗俗,还常常令人信服。

I dislike arguments of any kind.
They are always vulgar, and often convincing.

《不可儿戏》
The Importance of Being Earnest

73

《理想丈夫》
An Ideal Husband

自然是非常难摆的一种姿态。

To be natural is such a very difficult pose to keep.

我爱听别人的丑闻,对本人的可就兴味索然。
自己的丑闻缺乏新意。

**I love scandals about other people,
but scandals about myself don't interest me.
They have not got the charm of novelty.**

《道连·格雷的画像》
The Picture of Dorian Gray

75

《理想丈夫》
An Ideal Husband

现代生活中,没什么能比恰到好处的陈词滥调更有奇效。
一句好废话,天下成一家。

**In modern life nothing produces such
an effect as a good platitude.
It makes the whole world kin.**

理智的表情在哪里出现，美，真正的美就在哪里终结。
理智本身就是一种夸张，将脸部的和谐破坏殆尽。

Beauty, real beauty,
ends where an intellectual expression begins.
Intellect is in itself a mode of exaggeration
and destroys the harmony of any face.

《道连·格雷的画像》
The Picture of Dorian Gray

77

《对话》
In Conversation

我之前可能说过同样的事……但我确信，我的解释总在变化。

I may have said the same thing before …But my explanation, I am sure, will always be different.

人总能善待那些自己毫不在意的人。

One can always be kind to people about whom one cares nothing.

《道连·格雷的画像》
The Picture of Dorian Gray

79

《温夫人的扇子》
Lady Windermere's Fan

把人分为好坏,着实荒唐。人要么可爱,要么可厌。

It is absurd to divide people into good and bad.
People are whether charming or tedious.

越是去分析别人，就越失去分析的立场。
迟早要遭遇那无处不在的被称之为"人性"的可怕东西。

The more one analyses people,
the more all reasons for analysis disappear. Sooner or later
one comes to that dreadful universal thing called human nature.

《谎言的衰颓》
The Decay Of Lying

《社会主义制度下人的灵魂》
The Soul of Man Under Socialism

除了那些值得知道的事情之外,
大众对万事万物都有无法满足的好奇心。

The public have an insatiable curiosity to know everything,
except what is worth knowing.

我们每个人都是自己的恶魔，
联手把这个世界变成了我们的地狱。

We are each our own devil, and we make this world our hell.

《帕都瓦公爵夫人》
The Duchess of Padua

《道连·格雷的画像》
The Picture of Dorian Gray

摆脱诱惑的唯一途径是臣服于它。

The only way to get rid of temptation is to yield to it.

谁都能同情朋友的苦难，
但要感同身受朋友的成功却需要无比美好的品性。

Anybody can sympathize with the suffering of a friend,
but it requires a very fine nature to sympathize
with a friend's success.

《社会主义制度下人的灵魂》 The Soul of Man Under Socialism

85

《薇拉》
Vera

我宁可失去最亲密的朋友，也不愿失去最强劲的敌人。
要知道，一个人只要心地善良就会有朋友；
但倘若没有敌人，此人必定刻薄。

I would sooner lose my best friend than my worst enemy.
To have friends, you know, one need only be good-natured;
but when a man had no enemy left there
must be something mean about him.

仁义道德不过是我们针对自己讨厌的人所采取的态度。

Morality is simply the attitude we adopt
to people whom we personally dislike.

《理想丈夫》
An Ideal Husband

87

《身为艺术家的评论者》
The Critic as Artist

以真实面目表达时,最是言不由衷。
给他一张面具,他就会吐露真相。

Man is least himself when he talks in his own person.
Give him a mask, and he will tell you the truth.

些许真诚危险,太过真诚绝对致命。

A little sincerity is a dangerous thing,
and a great deal of it is absolutely fatal.

《身为艺术家的评论者》
The Critic as Artist

《道连·格雷的画像》
The Picture of Dorian Gray

充分实现自己的天性——是你我来人世走一遭的目的。

To realize one's nature perfectly –
that is what each of us is here for.

理想可是危险的东西。还是现实更好。现实伤人,但毕竟好些。

**Ideals are dangerous things. Realities are better.
They wound, but they're better.**

——《温夫人的扇子》 Lady Windermere's Fan

《身为艺术家的评论者》
The Critic as Artist

依照世俗的良善标准,做个好人显然轻而易举。
这仅仅需要一定程度猥琐的畏惧感、
一定程度欠缺的想象力以及一定程度对中产阶级体面的心若止水。

To be good, according to the vulgar standard of goodness,
is obviously quite easy.
It merely requires a certain amount of sordid terror,
a certain lack of imaginative thought,
and a certain low passion for middle-class respectability.

世人的同情心少一点,世间的麻烦也会少一点。

If there was less sympathy in the world there would be less trouble in the world.

《理想丈夫》
An Ideal Husband

《道连·格雷的画像》
The Picture of Dorian Gray

浅薄之辈需要历经数年方能挣脱一份情感。
收放自如之人终结悲伤就跟制造快乐一样易如反掌。

It is only shallow people who require years to get rid of an emotion.
A man who is master of himself can end a sorrow as
easily as he can invent a pleasure.

情绪不持久。这正是其主要魅力所在。

Moods don't last. It is their chief charm.

《无足轻重的女人》
A Woman of No Importance

95

《道连·格雷的画像》
The Picture of Dorian Gray

无论何时,一个人做出愚蠢透顶的事情来,往往是出于最高尚的动机。

**Whenever a man does a thoroughly stupid thing,
it is always from the noblest motives.**

顺其自然不过是装腔作势，
而且是我所知道的最惹人厌的装腔作势。

Being natural is simply a pose,
and the most irritating pose I know.

——《道连·格雷的画像》 *The Picture of Dorian Gray*

节制可是要人命的。适量就好比便饭一般寡淡。
过度才如盛宴一样尽兴。

Moderation is a fatal thing. Enough is as bad as a meal.
More than enough is as good as a feast.

罪恶这东西会自动显现于人脸，无可藏匿。

Sin is a thing that writes itself across a man's face.
It cannot be concealed.

《道连·格雷的画像》
The Picture of Dorian Gray

99

《温夫人的扇子》
Lady Windermere's Fan

我能抵抗住一切,除了诱惑。

I can resist everything except temptation.

世人所谓的不真诚，无非是丰富我们个性的一种手段。

What people call insincerity is simply a method by which we can multiply our personalities.

《身为艺术家的评论者》
The Critic as Artist

100

101

《供年轻人使用的至理名言》
Phrases and Philosophies for the Use of the Young

唯有肤浅之辈才了解自己。

Only the shallow know themselves.

没人富有到能够赎回自己的过去。

No man is rich enough to buy back his past.

《理想丈夫》
An Ideal Husband

《对话》
In Conversation

试图为世界做点什么的人总是让人难以忍受；
当世界为他们做了点什么时，他们则充满魅力。

Men who are trying to do something for the world,
are always insufferable,
when the world has done something for them,
they are charming.

人生过于重要,重要到不能严肃认真地加以谈论。

Life is much too important a thing ever to talk seriously about it.

——《薇拉》 *Vera*

《社会主义制度下人的灵魂》
The Soul of Man Under Socialism

"生活"是这个世界上最稀罕的东西。
大多数人只是存在,仅此而已。

To live is the rarest thing in the world.
Most people exist, that is all.

人生从来不是公平的……也许对我们大多数人而言，
不公平反倒是件好事。

Life is never fair … And perhaps it is a good thing
for most of us that it is not.

《理想丈夫》
An Ideal Husband

107

《道连·格雷的画像》
The Picture of Dorian Gray

我喜欢看戏。它比生活真实太多。

I love acting. It is so much real than life.

人应当吸收生活的色彩，但千万别记住细节。
细节往往庸俗不堪。

One should absorb the colour of life,
but one should never remember its details.
Details are always vulgar.

《道连·格雷的画像》
The Picture of Dorian Gray

然而过去不重要,现在也不重要。
我们不得不应对的是未来。因为过去是我们不该有的过去,
现在是我们不该在的现在。未来才属于艺术家。

But the past is of no importance.
The present is of no importance.
It is with the future that we have to deal.
For the past is what man should not have been.
The present is what man ought not to be.
The future is what artists are.

这世上只有两种悲剧：一种是事与愿违，另一种是得偿所愿。

**In this world there are only two tragedies.
One is not getting what one wants and the other is getting it.**

《温夫人的扇子》
Lady Windermere's Fan

111

《道连·格雷的画像》
The Picture of Dorian Gray

所有道路都通向同一个终点……幻灭。

All ways end at the same point ... disillusion.

突然发现自己一辈子讲的居然全是真话，
这对一个人来说着实可怕。

It is a terrible thing for a man to find out suddenly that
all his life he has been speaking nothing but the truth.

《不可儿戏》
The Importance of Being Earnest

《自深深处》
De Profundis

生活并不复杂,复杂的是我们。生活很简单,简单即正确。

**Life is not complex. We are complex. Life is simple,
and the simple thing is the right thing.**

人总该有点不可理喻之处。

One should always be a little improbable.

《供年轻人使用的至理名言》
Phrases and Philosophies for the Use of the Young

《温夫人的扇子》
Lady Windermere's Fan

这个世界上,我唯一想摸透的人就是我自己;
可眼下我看不出有这样的可能。

I am the only person in the world I should like to know thoroughly;
but I don't see any chance of it just at present.

要重返青春，你只消把以前干过的荒唐事再干一遍。

**To get back one's youth,
one has merely to repeat one's follies.**

《道连·格雷的画像》
The Picture of Dorian Gray

117

《英国的文艺复兴》
The English Renaissance of Art

我们每个人都在花时间寻找生活的秘密。
其实，生活的秘密就在艺术里。

We spend our days, each one of us,
in looking for the secret of life.
Well, the secret of life is in art.

差劲的艺术远比没有艺术要糟糕得多。

Bad art is a great deal worse than no art at all.

《居家装修》
House Decoration

119

《给艺术生的演讲》
Lecture to Art Students

……除了世人皆言不可为之事,再没有什么事情值得去做了。

... nothing is worth doing except what the world says is impossible.

出色的国王是现代民主政治唯一危险的敌人。

Good kings are the only dangerous enemies that modern democracy has.

——《薇拉》 Vera

121

《身为艺术家的评论者》
The Critic as Artist

我一向秉持这样的观点：执着是缺乏想象力最后的托辞……

I have always been of the opinion that consistency is the last refuge of the unimaginative ...

没什么能要了一位诗人的命,除了印刷错误。

A poet can survive everything but a misprint.

《诗人的孩子们》
The Children of the Poets

《身为艺术家的评论者》
The Critic as Artist

美洲永远都无法原谅欧洲,
因为历史上欧洲被发现的时间比它被发现的时间要早。

America has never quite forgiven Europe for having
been discovered somewhat earlier in history than itself.

一个人除非腰缠万贯,否则再有魅力也无处施展。
风流浪漫是有钱人的特权,不是无业游民的专长。
穷人应该脚踏实地、甘守本分。
有一份固定的收入强过迷人的气质。

Unless one is wealthy there is no use in being a charming fellow.
Romance is the privilege of the rich,
not the profession of the unemployed.
The poor should be practical and prosaic.
It is better to have a permanent income than to be fascinating.

《百万富翁模特》 The Model Millionaire

《夜莺与玫瑰》
The Nightingale and the Rose

倘若不能直言不讳,友谊的益处何在?
人人都会说动听的言语去取悦去奉承,
但真正的朋友说的永远是逆耳的忠言,不介意造成伤害。
确实,如果他是真朋友,他宁愿如此,因为他知道自己做得对。

But what is the good of friendship if
one cannot say exactly what one means?
Anybody can say charming things and try to please and to flatter,
but a true friend always says unpleasant things,
and does not mind giving pain. Indeed, if he is a really true friend,
he prefers it, for he knows that then he is doing good.

觉得旁人都远远不如自己，
这是唯一支撑人挨过此生的意念，
而我总是悉心培育这份意念。

The only thing that sustains one through life is the
consciousness of the immense inferiority of everybody else,
and this is a feeling that I have always cultivated.

《了不起的火箭》
The Remarkable Rocket

127

《了不起的火箭》
The Remarkable Rocket

我太过聪明，
以至于有时候连我本人都不明白自己在说些什么玩意。

I am so clever that sometimes
I don't understand a single word of what I am saying.

我向来秉持这样的观点：劳劳碌碌不过是无所事事者的救命稻草。

I have always been of opinion that hard work is simply the refuge of people who have nothing whatever to do.

——《了不起的火箭》 The Remarkable Rocket

《奥斯卡·王尔德警句》
The Epigrams of Oscar Wilde

祈祷应该永远得不到回应；否则就不成其为祈祷，而变成了通信。

**Prayer must never be answered: if it is,
it ceases to be prayer and becomes correspondence.**

哲学能教导我们泰然自若地接受邻居们的不幸。

Philosophy may teach us to bear with
equanimity the misfortunes of our neighbors...

《谎言的衰颓》
The Decay of Lying

我的个人经验是，越是深入地研究艺术，
越是浅显地关注自然……艺术是我们活力满满的抗议，
是我们力图让自然安分守己的勇敢尝试。

My own experience is that the more we study Art,
the less we care for Nature … Art is our spirited protest,
our gallant attempt to teach Nature her proper place.

思考是世上最不健康的事,人们死于思考,恰如死于疾病。
幸好,至少在英国,思考不会传染。

Thinking is the most unhealthy thing in the world,
and people die of it just as they die of any other disease.
Fortunately, in England at any rate, thought is not catching.

《谎言的衰颓》 The Decay of Lying

133

《谎言的衰颓》
The Decay of Lying

……模仿可以成为最实在的一种侮辱。

... imitation can be made the sincerest form of insult.

给出建议向来是傻事一桩，而给出好建议则绝对致命。
我希望你永远不犯这种错误，否则你会追悔莫及。

It is always a silly thing to give advice,
but to give good advice is absolutely fatal.
I hope you will never fall into that error. If you do,
you will be sorry for it.

《W.H. 先生的画像》
The Portrait of Mr. W. H

135

《W.H.先生的画像》
The Portrait of Mr. W. H

别忘了，一件事并不会因为有人为之丧命便必定是真的。

You forget that a thing is not necessarily
true because a man dies for it.

高谈阔论要么是无知者的矫揉造作，要么是精神空虚者的表白。

**Learned conversation is either the affectation of
the ignorant or the profession of the mentally unemployed.**

——《身为艺术家的评论者》
The Critic as Artist

《身为艺术家的评论者》
The Critic As Artist

任何人都可以创造历史。唯有伟人能书写历史。

Anybody can make history. Only a great man can write it.

交谈应当包罗万象,但又不着一物。

Conversation should touch everything
but should concentrate itself on nothing.

《身为艺术家的评论者》
The Critic as Artist

《道连·格雷的画像》
The Picture of Dorian Gray

书不存在所谓道德与不道德之分。
书只有写得好坏之别。仅此而已。

There is no such thing as a moral or an immoral book.
Books are well written, or badly written. That is all.

探入表层之下者风险自负。

Those who go beneath the surface do so at their peril.

《道连·格雷的画像》
The Picture of Dorian Gray

《道连·格雷的画像》
The Picture of Dorian Gray

一个你不再爱的人流露出的种种情感总会有些荒唐可笑。

**There is always something ridiculous about
the emotions of people whom one has ceased to love.**

自责也是一种享乐。当我们谴责自己时,
总觉得别人就无权责备我们了。赦免我们的是忏悔,不是神父。

**There is a luxury in self-reproach.
When we blame ourselves we feel that no
one else has a right to blame us. It is the confession,
not the priest, that gives us absolution.**

《道连·格雷的画像》
The Picture of Dorian Gray

《社会主义制度下人的灵魂》
The Soul of Man Under Socialism

当下,艺术决不该试图去迎合大众。
大众应努力去提升自身的美感。

Now Art should never try to be popular.
The public should try to make itself artistic.

艺术是世界上唯一严肃的事。而艺术家是唯一从来不严肃的人。

Art is the only serious thing in the world.
And the artist is the only person who is never serious.

《给过度教育者教学的几条格言》
A Few Maxims for the Instruction of the Over-Educated

145

《供年轻人使用的至理名言》
Phrases and Philosophies for the Use of the Young

邪恶是好人编造出来的概念,用以说明他人的奇妙魅力。

**Wickedness is a myth invented by good people
to account for the curious attractiveness of others.**

认为灵魂有别于肉体的人既无灵魂,也无肉体。

Those who see any difference between soul
and body have neither.

《供年轻人使用的至理名言》
Phrases and Philosophies for the Use of the Young

《供年轻人使用的至理名言》
Phrases and Philosophies for the Use of the Young

有抱负是失败的最后托辞。

Ambition is the last refuge of the failure.

爱自己是终生浪漫的肇始。

To love oneself is the beginning of a life-long romance.

《理想丈夫》
An Ideal Husband

《自深深处》
De Profundis

我的存在是一桩丑闻。

My existence is a scandal.

肉体之罪不值一提。它们是供医生治愈的病痛，
如果是该治的话。灵魂之罪才可耻。

Sins of the flesh are nothing.
They are maladies for physicians to cure,
if they should be cured. Sins of the soul alone are shameful.

《自深深处》
De Profundis

《自深深处》
De Profundis

……一切伟大的思想都是危险的。

... all great ideas are dangerous.

模仿在哪里终结,艺术就从哪里起步……

Art only begins where Imitation ends ...

——《自深深处》
De Profundis

153

《自深深处》
De Profundis

我生而特立独行,而非循规蹈矩。

I am one of those who are made for exceptions, not for laws.

我的品位最为简单。我从来只中意最好的。

I have the simplest tastes. I am always satisfied with the best.

《懒人印象》
An Idler's Impression

155

《温夫人的扇子》
Lady Windermere's Fan

人一旦老到懂事的年纪,他们就什么事都不懂了。

As soon as people are old enough to know better,
they don't know anything at all.

或许，人唯在粉墨登场时才最显从容。

Perhaps one never seems so much at one's ease as when one has to play a part.

《道连·格雷的画像》
The Picture of Dorian Gray

《王尔德致叶芝的书信》
A Letter to W.B.Yeats

我认为人应该创造自己的神话。

I think a man should invent his own myth.

没有伟大的艺术家是以事物的本来面貌去看待事物。
倘若如此，他就不再成其为艺术家。

No great artist ever sees things as they really are.
If he did would cease to be an artist.

《谎言的衰颓》
The Decay of Lying

对美的渴望不过是对生命渴望的升级版。

The desire for beauty is merely a heightened form of the desire for life.

按自己的意愿生活不是自私,
要求别人按自己的意愿生活才是自私。

**Selfishness is not living as one wishes to live,
it is asking others to live as one wishes to live.**

《身为艺术家的评论者》
The Critic as Artist

只有丧失理智的人才争论不休。

It is only the intellectually lost who ever argue.

信仰是乏味的。怀疑是让人沉迷的。
保持警醒是存活,自以为安全是死亡。

To believe is very dull. To doubt is intensely engrossing.
To be on the alert is to live, to be lulled into security is to die.

《对话》
In Conversation

《道连·格雷的画像》
The Picture of Dorian Gray

凡是我们感觉颠扑不破的事物从来都不是真的。
这是信仰的宿命,爱情的教训。

The things one feels absolutely certain about are never true.
That is the fatality of Faith, and the lesson of Romance.

恰恰因为一个人没能力做某件事，他才适宜当这件事的评判者。

It is exactly because a man cannot do
a thing that he is the proper judge of it.

《身为艺术家的评论者》
The Critic as Artist

《社会主义制度下人的灵魂》
The Soul of Man Under Socialism

在任何了解历史的人看来,不服从是人类的原始美德。
正是由于不服从——由于不服从和反叛——才有了进步。

Disobedience, in the eyes of anyone who has read history,
is man's original virtue.
It is through disobedience that progress has been made,
through disobedience and through rebellion.

社会常常放过罪犯,却从不宽恕梦想家。

Society often forgives the criminal;
it never forgives the dreamer.

《身为艺术家的评论者》
The Critic as Artist

167

《无足轻重的女人》
A Woman of No Importance

人生的奥秘在于永远不要怀着不得体的情感。

The secret of life is never to have an emotion that is unbecoming.

家庭是可怕的累赘,尤其是当人未婚时。

A family is s terrible encumbrance,
especially when one is not married.

《薇拉》
Vera

169

《薇拉》
Vera

常常有人活了多年,却仿佛死了一般,
然后突然所有的生活在一个时辰之内蜂拥而至。

One can live for years sometimes without living at all,
and then all life comes crowding into one single hour.

别跟我说你榨干了生活。一个人说出这话，
谁都知道是生活把他榨干了。

Don't tell me that you have exhausted life.
When a man says that one knows that life has exhausted him.

——《道连·格雷的画像》
The Picture of Dorian Gray

《无足轻重的女人》
A Woman of No Importance

所有的爱都是一场悲剧。

All love is a tragedy.

婚姻竟然就这样把一个男人给毁了！
跟香烟一样让人沦丧，代价还高昂得多。

How marriage ruins a man!
It's as demoralizing as cigarettes, and far more expensive.

——《温夫人的扇子》 *Lady Windermere's Fan*

《无足轻重的女人》
A Woman of No Importance

过度会带来无往不利的成功。

Nothing succeeds like excess.

你们这些追求始终如一的人,其实跟别人一样情绪繁杂。
唯一的区别在于你们的情绪没啥意义。

You people who go in for being consistent have
just as many moods as others have.
The only difference is that your moods are rather meaningless.

《道连·格雷的画像》
The Picture of Dorian Gray

《理想丈夫》
An Ideal Husband

我不喜欢原则……我更倾向偏见。

I don't like principles ... I prefer prejudices.

指望他人跟自己一样出类拔萃是不公平的。

It would be unfair to expect other people
to be as remarkable as oneself.

《了不起的火箭》
The Remarkable Rocket

《理想丈夫》
An Ideal Husband

只有无趣的人才会在早餐桌上出风头。

Only dull people are brilliant at breakfast.

婚姻的妙处之一是，让欺骗成为夫妻双方生活中的绝对必需。

The one charm of marriage is that it makes a life of deception absolutely necessary for both parties.

——《道连·格雷的画像》
The Picture of Dorian Gray

179

《帕都瓦公爵夫人》
The Duchess of Padua

**我看明白了,男人爱上女人,只把生命的一小部分献给她们,
而女人为了爱情会付出一切。**

**I see when men love women, they give them but a little of their lives.
But women when they love give everything.**

最恐怖的事情并不在于它会令人心碎——
心本就是用来碎的——而在于它让人心如磐石。

**The most terrible thing about it is not that it breaks one's heart—
hearts are made to be broken—but that it turns one's heart to stone.**

《自深深处》
De Profundis

图书在版编目(CIP)数据

迷人的气质:汉英对照/(英)奥斯卡·王尔德著;李玉瑶译.
-- 上海:上海文艺出版社,2022(2022.10重印)
ISBN 978-7-5321-8263-3

Ⅰ.①迷… Ⅱ.①奥…②李… Ⅲ.①英语-汉语-对照读物②格言-汇编-英国 Ⅳ.① H319.4:H

中国版本图书馆 CIP 数据核字(2021)第 274276 号

发 行 人　毕　胜
责任编辑　肖海鸥　李若兰
装帧设计　丁威静

书　　名　迷人的气质
作　　者　[英]奥斯卡·王尔德
译　　者　李玉瑶
出　　版　上海世纪出版集团　上海文艺出版社
地　　址　上海市闵行区号景路 159 弄 A 座 2 楼　201101
发　　行　上海文艺出版社发行中心
　　　　　上海市闵行区号景路 159 弄 A 座 2 楼 206 室　201101　www.ewen.co
印　　刷　北京中科印刷有限公司
开　　本　787×1092　1/40
印　　张　4.8
字　　数　20 千字
印　　次　2022 年 3 月第 1 版　2022 年 10 月第 2 次印刷
I S B N　978-7-5321-8263-3/I.6528
定　　价　52.00 元

告 读 者　如发现本书有质量问题请与印刷厂质量科联系　T: 021-37910000